Richard Scarry's
Best Bedtime Stories Ever

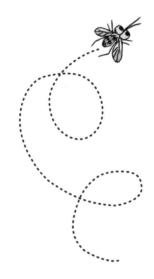

A Visit to the Big City, Mr Frumble's Bad Day and Down by the Busy Sea are all taken from Busiest People Ever. First published in Great Britain in 1976

A Spring Day and A Summer Picnic are taken from Great Big Air Book. First published in Great Britain in 1971

The counting exercise is taken from Best Counting Book Ever. First published in Great Britain in 1975

The Unlucky Day is taken from Funniest Storybook Ever. First published in Great Britain in 1972.

This edition published by HarperCollins Children's Books in 2011. HarperCollins Children's Books is a division of HarperCollins Publishers Ltd, 1 London Bridge Street, London SE1 9GF

12

ISBN: 978-0-00-741356-0

The HarperCollins website address is www.harpercollins.co.uk

Printed and bound in China

Richard Scarry's
Best Bedtime Stories Ever

HarperCollins *Children's Books*

A Spring Day

One spring morning a breeze blew a feather through the bedroom window.

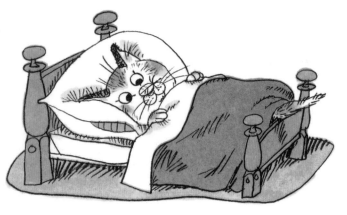

It tickled Huckle's nose.
"Aaah-chooo!" sneezed Huckle.

Huckle sneezed so hard that he blew Little Sister out of bed.
"Oh it must be windy today!" she said.

Huckle and Little Sister are breathing in
the fresh morning air.
Then they blow it out again.

You do it too. Breathe in! Breathe out!
When you blow out, you make the air move.
You make a little wind of your own.

After breakfast, Miss Honey, the schoolteacher, stopped by to take the children for
a walk in the spring air. A strong wind came in the door with her.

It was a very windy day.
The children felt the wind pushing against them.
"Look at all the things the wind does," said Miss Honey.
"It makes the waves on the sea. It makes the clouds move and
the trees sway. It even dries the clothes on the clothesline."

The air becomes warmer in the springtime.
There is a sweet smell from the flowers and bugs fly back and
forth through the air. Flower seeds float on the spring breezes.
Colourful kites fly high in the sky.

Narcissus

Crocus

Lowly
Worm

Tulip

Daffodil

Violet

Lily of
the Valley

Some people like to go for a drive
in the fresh spring air.

Dandelion

Farmer Fox ploughs his field for spring planting.
The plough loosens the soil so air and water can get in.
The roots of growing plants will need air and water.

"Oh, oh! It's going to rain," said Farmer Fox.
"My new tractor will get all wet.
Oops! I just felt a drop. I must hurry for shelter."

"Hurry, Mother Cat! Your laundry will get wet too.
Hurry everyone! We must help Mummy bring the
laundry into the house before it gets wet!"

Farmer Fox brought in Mummy's laundry just in time. He brought in his tractor too!
The laundry didn't get wet, and neither did his tractor.
Everyone gathered around to have tea and cocoa and cookies while waiting for the rain to stop.

In the kitchen Miss Honey had something else to show them.
"We all felt the big wind blowing outdoors today," she said.
"But right now, in this kitchen, a little wind is blowing."
Miss Honey pointed to the small clouds rising from the spout
of the teakettle. Hot, steaming air was coming out of it.
"Hot air always rises," said Miss Honey.
"The hot, steaming air from the teakettle is making
a tiny wind right here in the kitchen!"

A Visit to the Big City

Mother Cat is taking Huckle and Lowly to the city.
What do you think they are going to do there?
They have to take the train. Mother Cat sits in the passenger
coach. Huckle and Lowly sit with the driver of the engine.
TO-O-O-O-t! Lowly pulls the whistle. Off they go.

bulb changer

taxi driver

travelling salesman

skier

scout leader

porter

scouts

mountain climber

waiter

cook

Mother Cat

signalman

passengers

DINING CAR

COACH

wheel tapper

BUSYTOWN

TICKETS

TIME TABLE

NEWSPAPERS

BAGGA

ticket seller

newsdealer

baggage
checker

fork-lift truck
operator

sandwich eater

station master

snack-cart attendant

conductor

oiler

truck driver

bricklayer

mechanical shovel

plumber

carpenters

bulldozer operator

bricklayer

plumber

HOUSES FOR SALE

mortar mixer

bathtub deliverymen

driver

newspaper reader

carpenters

electrician

roofer

painter

paper-hanger

nail spiller

gardener

stove and refrigerator
deliveryman

SOLD

TV

The train chugs along the tracks on
the way to the big city.
Suddenly Lowly shouts, "STOP! Something is wrong!"
The train stops. Lowly jumps down from the
locomotive and runs to the switch.
What can the matter be?

driver

school-bus driver

SCHOOL BUS

log cutter

log hauler

tree chopper

kite flier

vagrant

grass mower

TV

A goods train is speeding towards them on the same line.
Lowly moves the switch … just in time! The goods train rolls onto
another line. Lowly has saved everyone from a terrible accident.
Lowly is certainly a good railway worker, isn't he?

Watch out,
Mr. Frumble!

ICE
CREAM

TRAVEL GIFT SHOP LEFT LUGGAGE FLOWERS

FLY

COME TO LAND

MAIL

PLATFORM 3

luggage trolley driver

PLATFORM 2

sleeping-car

workers running to catch their train

sweeper

PLATFORM 1

SNACK BAR

NEWSAGENT

window cleaner

TV

clock fixer

EXIT

jewellery seller

TICKETS

TIMETABLE

TO TAXIS

porter

pencil seller

Finally the train arrives at the city's railway station.
What a big, busy place it is!
Look! Someone is there to greet
the three arrivals. Who can he be?

steel workers

nosy pedestrian

welder

crane operator

foreman

cement mixer

NOW BUILDING
A NEW
SKYSCRAPER

TV1

A television producer has come to meet them.
A few days ago he had invited Huckle and
Lowly to appear on his television show.
He drives them through the city streets
to the television studio.

In the television studio, Huckle and Lowly sing a jolly song. People all over the country can see and hear the programme on their television sets.

When Huckle and Lowly return to Busytown, all their friends will tell them that they saw the programme, too.

Grandma Cat lives far away, but she sees Huckle and Lowly on her television set. She is very surprised and pleased. "I must visit my two television entertainers soon," she says. Would YOU like to be a television singer, too?

A Summer Picnic

It was a bright, sunny summer day. There was not a cloud in the sky.
Miss Honey and her boyfriend, Bruno, decided to take all the children on a picnic.

They drove past a lake where
some fishermen were fishing.
Oh, oh! They seem to have caught something!

While they were setting out the picnic, Rudolf von Strudel,
the famous airplane pilot, dropped by.
"Miss Honey!" he said. "A big thunderstorm is coming this way!
You and the children must take shelter immediately!"

SCHOOL BUS

Ants always
come to picnics!

Everyone had been too busy putting out food to
notice the black storm clouds gathering in the sky.
"Hurry!" Rudolf warned. "The rain will start any minute."

C-r-a-a-a-a-a-c-c-k-k-k!
The lightning flashed! The thunder roared!
But everyone was safely inside the school bus.

No one got even the tiniest bit wet.
Not even Farmer Fox's tractor.
It was the best rainy-day picnic ever.

Mr. Frumble's Bad Day

Mr. Frumble is going to work. He forgot to open the garage doors before he backed the car. What a bad way to start the day!

butcher

cashier

manager

There are a few things Mr. Frumble must do on his way to work. First, he stops to shop at the supermarket. Look at what he's done now!

book borrowers

librarian

Next, he goes to the library to borrow a book.
The librarian does not like noisy sneezers.

barber

At the barber shop he fidgets so much that the
barber cuts his tie by mistake.

chemist

Mr. Frumble has a little accident when he buys
some vitamins from the chemist.

Then he tries on a suit at the clothing store.
"I think you need a larger size, Mr. Frumble."

He tries on a hat.
"Don't pull it down so hard, Mr. Frumble."

laundrette attendant

He washes his laundry at the laundromat.
"I think you have put too much soap in the machine, Mr. Frumble."

nurse

At Dr. Lion's office he breaks the scales. Does Mr. Frumble weigh THAT much?

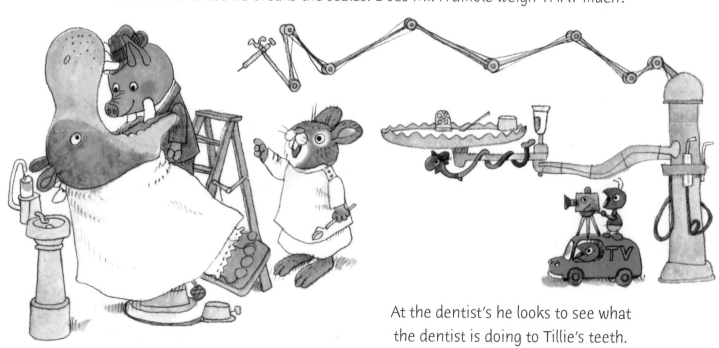

At the dentist's he looks to see what
the dentist is doing to Tillie's teeth.
"Please sit down and wait your turn, Mr. Frumble."

Mr. Frumble goes into a restaurant to eat his lunch.
He sees the chef cooking some Flambéed Bananas.

Mr. Frumble thinks the fire is dangerous.
He throws water on it.

The chef is furious.
"I NEED fire to cook my Bananas," he says.
"Now you have ruined them."

The angry chef frightens Mr. Frumble. He runs out of the restaurant.
Oops! Watch where you are going, Mr. Frumble.

DRIVE-IN BANK

bank teller

SCHOOL

teacher

pupils

Bananamobile driver

STOP

POST OFFICE

post-office clerk

Mr. Frumble gets back into his car, but again he doesn't look where he is going. He runs into a water hydrant and accidentally puts out another fire on the chef's Flaming Bananas.

newsboy

photographer

TV

reporter

THE DAILY EAGLE

typist

editor

MUSIC SHOP

RESTAURANT

OUR SPECIALITY—
FLAMBÉED BANANAS

chimney sweep

AUTOMOBILES

BICYCLES

THE COFFEE POT

COFF

car salesman

newspaper deliveryman

NEWSPAPER DELIVERY

linotype operator

printers

bulldozer operator

bugdozer operator

road layer

dump-truck driver

PETROL

Mr. Frumble! How did you ever get your car on that new road?
It's not ready yet for drivers. The workers are still busy building it.
Get off immediately. You have certainly had a bad day,
haven't you, Mr. Frumble?

pumpkin-car driver

petrol pump attendant

car greaser

road-roller operator

dump-truck driver

SOS

"It's about time you went home," Lowly tells Mr. Frumble, "before you cause any more trouble. I will call a breakdown truck for you."

pilot

breakdown truck driver

A breakdown truck comes and takes Mr. Frumble home. So long, Mr. Frumble. You didn't even get to work today. Maybe things will be better tomorrow.

lightship captain

tugboat skipper

crane operator

helmsman

ship's captain

lobster fisherman

straddle-carrier driver

fork-lift truck driver

TAXI

TAXI

taxi driver

Down by the Busy Sea

coastguard

radio operator

waiter

purser

passengers

ship's painter

Huckle and Lowly are visiting Captain Salty down at the pier.
The captain shows them all the things there are to see at a harbour.
"This is a passenger ship," he explains. "It will carry people across the ocean
to visit their friends in distant places."
Lowly thinks *he* would like to be a sea captain when he grows up.

lighthouse keeper

sailor

fishermen

Next, Captain Salty points to a cargo ship.
"It can carry all kinds of things to distant ports," he says.
"Just now cars are being loaded into its hold. The ship will carry them
across the sea, and people in far-away countries will drive them."
"LOOK!" cries Captain Salty loudly.
"There is a fire on that barge. We must help!
Hop onto the fire-tender. Let's go!"

captain

stevedores

fire-tender
captain

fork-lift truck driver

harbour police

giant-crane operator

dockside train driver

submarine skipper

Mr. Frumble, the boat wrecker

The fire-tender rushes towards the burning barge and sprays it with water.

TV

FERRY

ferry-boat captain

fire-tender firemen

lazy fisherman

Captain Tillie has jumped off the burning barge.
"Help! Help!" she cries.
Lowly jumps overboard with a life-belt to save her.

A wet Captain Tillie thanks Lowly and gives
him a big kiss. Isn't it amazing that such a little
fellow can rescue such a big sea captain?
Good work, Sea Captain Lowly.

The Unlucky Day

Mr. Raccoon opened his eyes. "Wake up, Mamma," he said. "It looks like a good day."

He turned on the water. The tap broke off. "Call Mr. Fixit, Mamma," he said.

He sat down to breakfast. He burned his toast. Mamma burned his bacon.

Mamma told him to bring home food for supper. As he was leaving, the door fell off its hinges.

Driving down the road, Mr. Raccoon had a flat tyre.

While he was changing it, his trousers ripped.

He started again. His car engine exploded and wouldn't go any farther.

He decided to walk. The wind blew his hat away. Bye-bye, hat!

While chasing after his hat,
he fell into a manhole.

Then he climbed out and bumped
into a lamp post.

A policeman yelled at him for
bending the lamp post.

"I must be more careful," thought Mr. Raccoon.
"This is turning into a bad day."

He didn't look where he was going.
He bumped into Mrs. Rabbit and broke
all her eggs.

Another policeman gave him a ticket for
littering the pavement.

His friend Warty Warthog came up
behind him and patted him on the back.
Warty! Don't pat so hard!
"Come," said Warty. "Let's go to a
restaurant for lunch."

Warty ate and ate and ate. Have you ever seen such bad table manners? Take off your hat, Warty!

Warty finished and left without paying for what he had eaten. Mr. Raccoon had to pay for it. Just look at all the plates that Warty used!

The lunch cost Mr. Raccoon every penny he had with him. "What other bad things can happen to me today?" he wondered.

Well... for one thing, the tablecloth could catch on his belt buckle!

"Don't you ever come in here again!" the waiter shouted.

"I think I had better go home as quickly as possible," thought Mr. Raccoon. "I don't want to get into any more trouble."

He arrived home just as Mr. Fixit was leaving. Mr. Fixit had spent the entire day finding new leaks. "I will come back tomorrow to fix the leaks," said Mr. Fixit.

Mrs. Raccoon asked her husband if he had brought home the food she asked for. She wanted to cook something hot for supper. Of course Mr. Raccoon hadn't, so they had to eat cold pickles for supper.

After supper they went upstairs to bed. "There isn't another unlucky thing that can happen to me today," said Mr. Raccoon as he got into bed. Oh, dear! His bed broke! I do hope that Mr. Raccoon will have a better day tomorrow, don't you?

Willy Bunny Learns to Count

1 one

Here is Willy Bunny. Willy is ONE bunny. Here comes Sally Bunny on her scooter.
Now there are two bunnies. Both bunnies have two eyes, two hands, two feet and two long ears.

2 two

One mother and one father make two parents. Two fried eggs make a good breakfast for Daddy. Can you count two of anything else?

3 three

Willy and Sally go outside to play.
Along comes their friend, Freddy Bunny.
Two bunnies and one bunny make three bunnies.
How many wheels are on Freddy's tricycle?
That's right! There are three wheels.

"Look at the three trucks," says Willy.
"One is big and two are small."

4 four

Here comes Flossie Bunny with her wagon.
Three bunnies and one bunny make four bunnies. Now there are two girl bunnies and two boy bunnies. Flossie has brought four apples in her four-wheeled wagon for everyone to share.

Four mouse buses go down the street. Two are yellow and two are red.

5 five

Beep-beep. Here comes Joey on his go-cart.
That makes five bunnies. Four were here
already, and one more makes five.

Four of the bunnies hear their
mothers calling them home.
That leaves just one bunny – Willy.
But Willy doesn't mind being alone.
He still has lots of things to count.
He sees five racing cars.

"One, two, three, four,
five," he counts.

6 six

Ding! Ding! Ding! Ding! Ding! Ding!
Five fire engines and a fire chief's car are
speeding down the street. That makes six in
the fleet. Three have ladders. Three do not.
Five are red and one is white.
Where is the fire?

7 seven

The fire must be in the Cat family's farmhouse. Seven cats are running out of the house.
Five are dressed and ready for school. The other two are a mother and a baby.

8 eight

The fire is in Mother Cat's oven, where she is baking eight pies. Five pies are burned, but three are baked just right. They did get a little wet, though. How many cats are going to eat at the table?

9 nine

Well, those firemen have certainly made a mess of Mother Cat's kitchen floor.

Splish! Splosh! Splash!

They clean up with nine mops. Five mops are red, two are green and two are yellow.

10 ten

Here comes Father Cat with ten watermelons from his garden. He slips and half of them fly out of his basket. Five watermelons are still safe in his basket.

Who has caught the sixth, seventh, eighth and ninth melons?
Will Mother Cat be able to catch the tenth one before it falls to the ground?
Look out, Mother Cat!

Now let us see what Willy has counted so far.

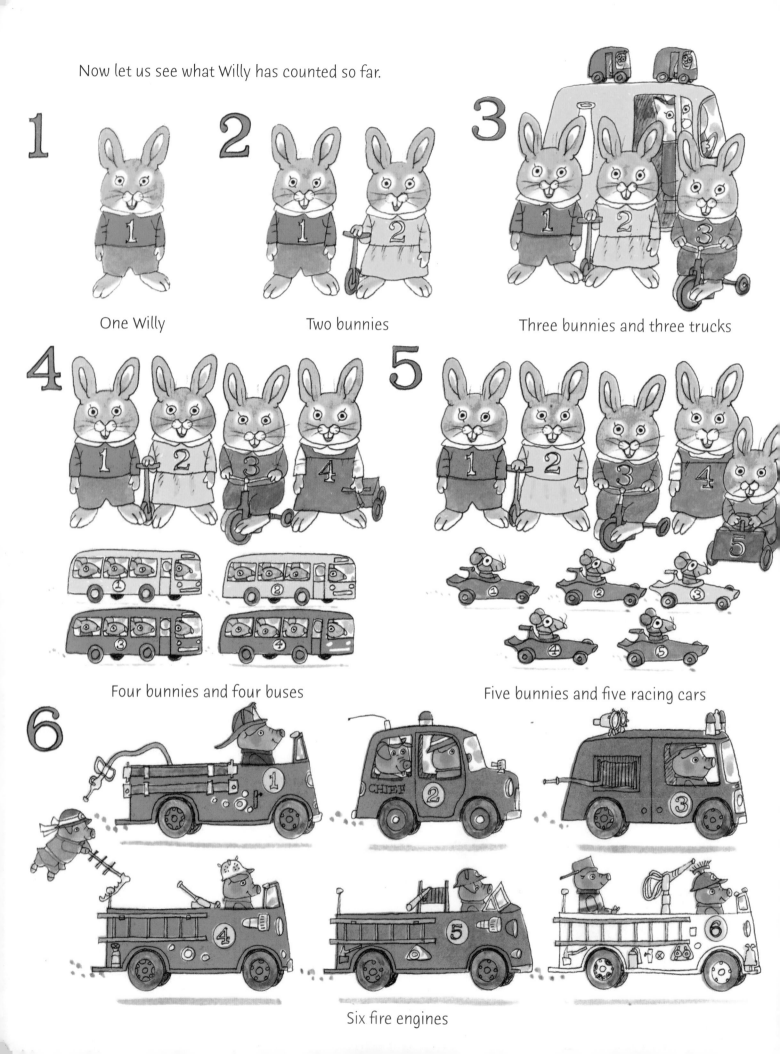

1 One Willy

2 Two bunnies

3 Three bunnies and three trucks

4 Four bunnies and four buses

5 Five bunnies and five racing cars

6 Six fire engines

7 Seven cats

8 Eight pies

9 Nine mops

10 Nine melons, and the one that
Mother Cat caught, makes ten melons.
Good for her!

100 one hundred

After supper, Willy and his father go outside. Willy counts one hundred fireflies glowing in the dark sky. It looks as if the fireflies can count to one hundred, too.

And so can you!
Good night!

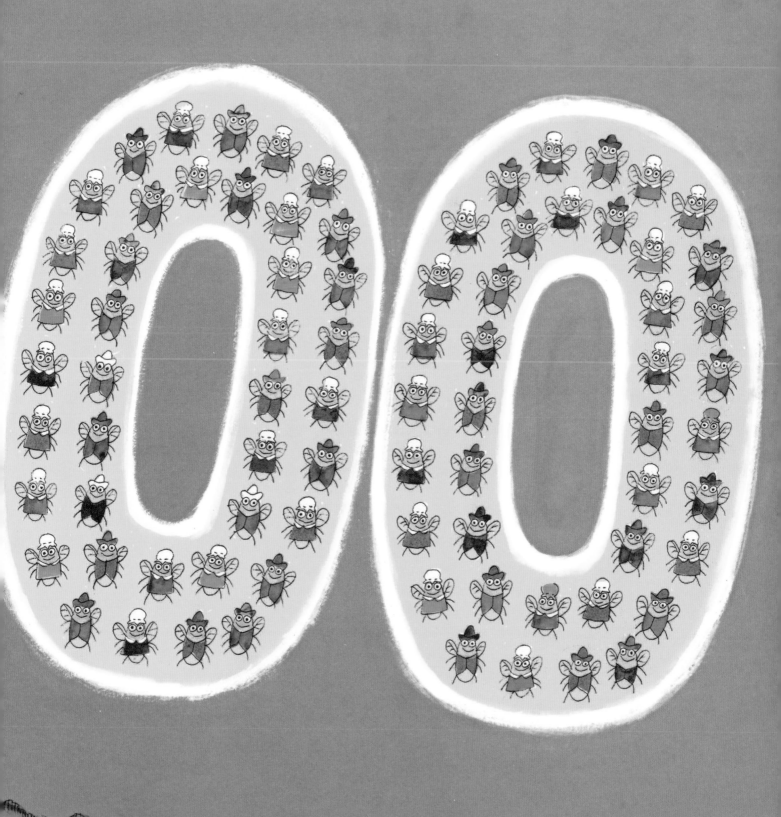